ANNA
ANGRYSAURUS

Written by
Brian Moses

Illustrated by
Mike Gordon

BARRON'S

Anna Angrysaurus always seemed
to be angry about something.

Sometimes she got angry when she couldn't watch her favorite program on television. "Why do we have to watch a silly tailball game? I hate tailball."

Sometimes she got angry when her brother or sister received a present and she didn't.

"But Anna, you got a present last week when you did well at school," her Mom said.

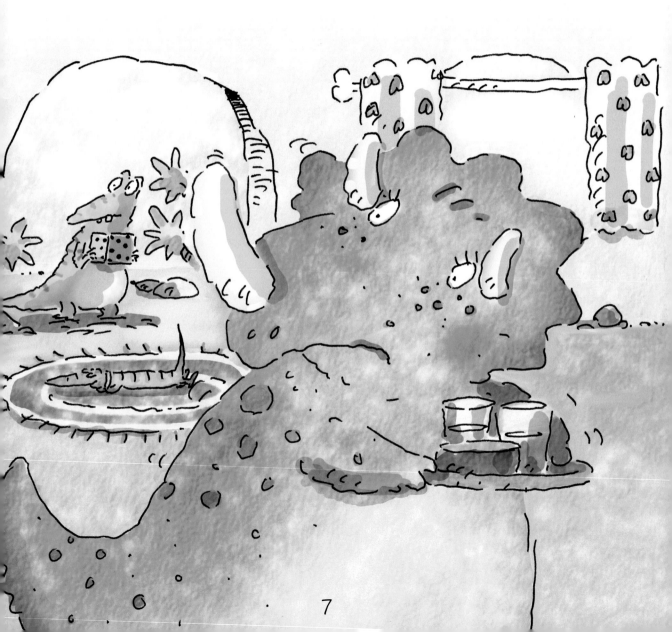

Sometimes she got angry when her brother won a game of "Who can stick his or her head in a T. Rex's mouth?"

"But Anna, you win that game most times.
It's good for your brother if he
wins occasionally."

Sometimes she got angry and nobody knew why she was angry. Even Anna didn't seem to know why she was angry.

When that happened, she often
charged at the door.

Later, she felt sorry because it made her look silly!

Anna often ROARED or HOWLED when she was angry.

Sometimes she ROARED so loudly that the windows rattled and stuff fell off shelves.

Or Anna would stamp her feet
when she was angry and cause
wavy lines to appear on
the television.

"I wish you wouldn't do that," her Dad called out. "I'm trying to watch the Dinoworld News."

"I'm sorry," Anna said. "But when I get really angry, I can't stop myself."

"I feel just like one of the volcanoes that we can see from our windows. I know I'm ready to explode."

"Anna, sometimes the things you forget to do make me angry," her Mom said. "I'm thinking about when you spill your paints on the carpet and leave me to clean up the mess."

"But I try to stay calm by counting to ten or by taking deep breaths before I say anything. I don't charge at the door."

"And it makes me angry," said Anna's Dad, "when you and your brother and sister can't play together without calling each other silly names."

"But it helps me calm down
if I count to ten before telling
you to stop."

"Next time you start to feel angry,"
Anna's Mom told her, "try
closing your eyes
and counting to five.
That might help."

24

"Or think about the things you do well or enjoy. That might help you forget your angry feelings."

"You could also try talking to us about why you get so angry," her Mom said.

"I used to lose my temper a lot when I was a young dinosaur," her Dad said. "I know how you feel."

So the next time Anna felt as if she were
a pterodactyl egg about to crack open, or
a balloon about to burst, she stopped, thought
for a bit, and then roared...

...but much
more quietly
than usual.

"That's much better," her Dad said.
"Maybe now we can get a new front door."

NOTES FOR PARENTS AND TEACHERS

Read the book with children either individually or in groups.
Talk to them about what makes them angry. How do they feel
when they are angry? Do they recognize any of the things that
make Anna angry?

How would they picture themselves getting angry? Would it be
an erupting volcano, a charging bull, or something else?
Perhaps they can draw how they picture themselves.

Help children to compose short poems that focus on their
own angry feelings:

> I feel angry when my brother is given candy and I don't get any.
> I feel angry when somebody steps on my toe and doesn't
> say sorry.
> I feel angry when I break a favorite toy.
> I feel angry...

Ask children if there are some things that made them angry that
they realized afterwards weren't worth getting angry about.
How did they feel when they had calmed down and looked back
on what made them angry?

There are strategies in this book for helping children to control their
anger. Can they identify what these are? How effective do the
children think they would be? Do children have their own ways
of calming themselves down?

For example:

I imagine myself as a balloon and then suddenly the air whooshes out.

I imagine myself as a storm that gradually fades away.

I imagine myself as a raging river that calms down to a gentle flow.

Look at other words and phrases for angry—furious, snarl, snap, fume, rage, losing your temper, throwing a tantrum, hopping mad. Ask children to write short sentences that include these words and phrases.

Sometimes children's behavior can make other people angry. Ask them to think about what would make parents angry. What would make teachers angry? Can children think of recent examples where their own behavior has made someone else angry?

Talk about how the actions of thoughtless people can affect others—a dog cutting its paw on broken glass, litter left around in the countryside. Are these the sort of things that could make someone angry?

Explore the notion of anger further through the sharing of picture books mentioned in the book list on page 32.

BOOKS TO SHARE

Is It Right to Fight?: A First Look at Anger   Pat Thomas
Explores why it's better to resolve conflicts without screaming, hitting, or using other expressions of anger.

I Can Make A Difference: A First Look at Setting a Good Example
Pat Thomas
Emotions like anger take a back seat when we treat others the way we'd like to be treated.

Sometimes I'm a...Monster   Gillian Shields,
Illustrated by Georgie Birkett
All children have moments when they are sweet angels...and others when they are little monsters!

Sometimes I Feel...Sunny   Gillian Shields,
Illustrated by Georgie Birkett
Explores the emotions that kids go through, from feeling sunny and brave to being sad and grumpy.

My Manners Matter: A First Look at Being Polite   Pat Thomas
Showing kindness makes working and playing together better for everyone.